William Joseph Ibbett

Little Poems of a Poeticule

William Joseph Ibbett

Little Poems of a Poeticule

ISBN/EAN: 9783337408626

Printed in Europe, USA, Canada, Australia, Japan

Cover: Foto ©Andreas Hilbeck / pixelio.de

More available books at **www.hansebooks.com**

LITTLE POEMS

OF

A POETICULE

BY

ANTÆUS

LONDON
PRINTED FOR THE AUTHOR

TO MRS. NOBODY.

I DEDICATE this book to you. I did intend to offer it to my wife, but her thoughts run so much on shirts and shifts, dinners and babies, and fal-lals of that sort, that I really love you better than her.

CONTENTS.

ON MY BOOK.

Who'll read my verse? God knows! I don't!
But I can point the men who won't.
The sour and stiff who's quick to hate
His neighbour from a jealous pate,
And drones in learnéd accents slow
How great the bard who's steeped in woe—
A common city man will love
Me better than this vicious dove.
The men that pray, the men that preach
At British sin would only retch
If they were made to chant my verse
That they with priggish instinct curse.
Who'll read it then? God only knows,
But here it is in printed rows,
Made by myself in vacant hours,
When cold or darkness hid the flowers,

B

For all who fear not to incline
Their hearts to what's not very fine,
But only tells of things that all
Have seen or done in Common Hall.

MARY.

Is this laughing lass named Mary?
Doleful name for such a fairy—
Name of sweet and sighing sadness,
Wan lament and gentle madness!

But this girl has eyes so bright,
Veiled with softness, armed with might,
That they make the dullest swain
Long for one quick glance again.

And she has lips of reddest hue,
Lips that pout when pouts are due,
Made for kisses warm and soft,
Kisses long and kisses oft.

And she has words that quick dispel
Morbid thoughts and fancies fell ;
It is true that they are small,
But they mean Love, and Love is all.

To the graces of a fairy
Give no more the name of Mary.
Mary is but rampant folly ;
She is darling, charming Polly.

MAUD.

A WOULD-BE brazen lass is she,
Spurning sighs deliciously,
Pelting love with gibing fun,
Though she's barely twenty-one.

She laughs at all I do and say ;
She flouts me through the live-long day,
And calls my two and thirty years
Brave sentinels against her fears.

But when I kiss her mocking face
What makes her silent leave the place,
Both her cheeks a burning red,
All her pretty scornings dead?

LAST NIGHT.

A LOVE LETTER.

ON your brow the heather lay
　　True and red, true and red.
How I coveted the spray!
　　But you fled, but you fled
Ere I found the heart to say
　　The unsaid, the unsaid.

Then I searched a weary hill
　　For the flower, many an hour;
But the shifty moon's ill-will,
　　Chaste and sour, hid the flower.

Yet the eyebright glistened clear
  All the time, empty time ;
So I plucked it for its cheer
  Out of thyme, scented thyme,
And I wrap it for my dear
  In a rhyme, wistful rhyme.

YOUTH SUPINE.

You little birds that soar above
  The golden flowers that deck the field,
Know that, howe'er you sing, my love
  Hath frowned and will not yield.

And yet, as I lie on the sward
  At love and all things murmuring,
Because my lady dear is hard,
  You dare to soar and sing !

But wait until the rose's hue
  Hath sprinkled every hedge along,

Then she shall come with me to you
And smile at your proud song.

For every day I'll ask her grace,
And every day I'll faithful prove,
So shall she turn at last her face
To me with gentle love ;

And sit just here, you noisy elves,
And call you all a rattling toy,
Not half as happy as ourselves
Who cannot sing for joy.

THE BETTER PART.

YOU dames that tread the stony way
With solemn face and clothing gay,
And mien that damns your fine array,
Have vexed me sore :

But now there is across the mead
A better book for me to read,
A loving little girl indeed,
    That I love more.

First, far away beneath the trees
An apron flutters in the breeze,
A snowy sign to him who sees
    To haste and kiss ;

And when I shout and mend my pace,
She comes towards with laughing face,
And meets me with a dainty grace
    Foretelling bliss.

'Tis now we search each other's eyes
To find for sure the grandest prize,
That makes us tremble with surprise
    And stand stock still.

And if we happen on a stile
She hides her legs with pretty wile,
And plays at touch-me-not with smile
    That loves my will.

But when the sun sets, then we know
That we may clutch at things below,
And cease to care for vanished show
    Of prudish day.

So as she pants I fold her tight,
And we forget the things of light,
And in the dark begin Love's rite
    Without delay.

But what you ladies in a bed
Of sweaty linen bear in dread,
We do within a scented shed
    Of wild woodbine.

And last, when time comes to depart,
She cries because it's hard to part,
But with a tender, happy heart,
    This girl of mine.

HE'S BUT A SILLY WOOER.

HE'S but a silly wooer,
Yet must he still pursue her,
    A lady gay
    Who loves to stray
    Through field and meadow all the day.

His love can never bind her,
Nor weary footstep find her :
    He sees her fair,
    With ribboned hair,
    Far, far away ; but if he dare

Too near, with shouts of laughter
She flees, and he goes after
    To watch her fade,
    A mocking shade,
    Adown the windings of a glade.

She's small as Mab and madder
Than he, tho' he is sadder,
 So far to go,
 In wistful woe
 Till down he sinks in brambles low,

Nor heeds their bloody stickle
Nor brier's cruel prickle,
 That do but lie
 As carelessly
 As one who's fallen fain to die.

SERENADE.

Rise, my girl, and now be keeping
 Love's bespangled holiday ;
Kisses gender if their reaping
 Fall beneath bright Vesper's ray.
Single boys and girls are sleeping
 Deaf and dumb, a cloddish nay ;
Widowed lovers lie a-weeping
 For the loves they've lost to-day.

TO NANNY.

Every lively thing is pining
   For the kindness of a mate ;
Let us then, each other twining,
   Feed on love and laugh at Fate—
Fate that's ever darkly mining
   Through the way of age and hate,
So shall we, on kisses dining,
   Meet it in our festal state.

TO NANNY.

You know you said—it was not I—
That Life is short and we must die
Too soon, and yet you still defy
   My fond embraces.

You saw the sun this very day
Drive o'er its semi-circled way
And set at last, nor would delay
   Its final graces.

They say it's sure to come again
To-morrow just to shine on men
And women for their joy ; but then
　　Are you so certain ?

If you are not, take present bliss
By very token of the kiss
That I would give, and never miss
　　For all night's curtain.

But if you are, it 'll surely shine
On wistful hearts, as yours and mine,
Tho' others will be beating fine
　　With hope that's founded

On what they 've done before, while we
Shall bear it's brightness heavily,
And sigh in vain for what might be
　　If you abounded.

In love of what your neighbours do,
In faith in me who wait and sue
For what is old, but ever new
　　To all things living.

Then, Nanny, be not coy nor run
From him you love, nor seek to shun
The joy that blesses everyone
    Who's quick in giving.

CHORUS OF SOLDIERS

AT THE MARRIAGE OF THEIR GENERAL.

To the town, mates, sing around,
    Little shoes and frocks to buy :
Little feet are near the ground ;
    Camp shall hear the babies cry.

What care we for toil and sorrow ?
    Little faces won't be long
Filling out the glad to-morrow,
    Like their fathers, with a song.

Women's smiles and brave men's laughter
    Meeting end in babies' eyes ;
Babes shall be big men hereafter,
    Say the wisest of the wise.

YOUTH.

A LITTLE child was walking down
    The garden path one April day,
And spied a pear-tree's snowy crown,
    The tiny bush's sole display.

He laughed to see the pretty sight,
    And stretched his hand to seize the toy,
When mother, heedful of the right,
    Cried, " Pluck it not, you naughty boy!
The fruit will give you more delight—
    The blossom's but a fleeting joy."

The child said naught, but sly and gay
    He plucked, and stole within a bower
Where he might sit at ease and play
    With those white virgins for an hour.

TO A CHILD.

LAST April prime you called me fool,
　And now you bring me roses:
Dear little lass, what is your rule
　For floutings and for posies?

If you were older you might say
　"To everything its season,"
But you're so young, your tiny way
　Slips under age's reason.

And yet both times you laughed and kissed
　My black beard in this meadow,
Where youths shall sigh because they've missed
　The sight of e'en your shadow.

Maybe the sun fell on my face
　And made it bright as any:—
But sin it is to probe your grace;
　I'll cheer it with a penny.

CHRISTMAS.

HOLLY berries red,
  Missel berries white,
And a maiden's face
  Make a Christmas right.

Missel berries white
  And a maiden's face,
Laughing in the glow,
  Make a kissing case.

And a maiden's face,
  After being kissed,
Goes away to hide
  Till by all it's missed.

O, we cry, she's kissed
  And has gone to hide,
She will soon come back
  Blushing like a bride.

Long she cannot hide,
  For she loves the light,
Reddens as she comes
  Back to bonny bright.

As she comes to light,
  Hanging down her head,
Berries like her face
  Mix their white and red.

Holly berries red,
  Missel berries white,
And a maiden's face
  Make a Christmas right.

FUNEREAL.

To the earth with a dearth
  Of babbling speech we bare him:
Meanest shroud, for a crowd
  Of grovelling worms shall share him.

D

Silent stand, a trembling band
   On the ogre mother ;
Look with awe into her maw ;
   All shall fill no other.

Lay him low ; end the show ;
   Strip him of his trappings.
Naked earth at his birth,
   Needs he now no wrappings.

Come away! Why delay?
   Clay is dull and heavy.
Old is she. Children, we
   Dance in fleeting bevy.

WATERSHED.

Now on Life's crest we breathe the temperate air.
   Turn either way ! The parted path o'erlook !
Dear, we shall never bid the Sphinx despair,
   Nor read in Sibyl's book.

The blue bends o'er us; good are night and day;
   Some blissful influence of the starry seven
Thrilled us ere youth took wing : why now essay
   The vain assault on heaven?

And what great word Life's singing lips pronounce,
   And what intends the sealing kiss of Death,
It skills us not; yet we accept, renounce,
   And draw this tranquil breath.

Enough, one thing we know; haply anon
   All truths, yet no truth better or more clear
Than that your hand holds my hand; therefore, on!
   The downward pathway, Dear.

                           EDWARD DOWDEN.

LINES WRITTEN AFTER READING THE FOREGOING.

I KNOW the Sphinx has long laid with the dead,
   And Sibyl only wrote to send astray ;
'Tis to kind eyes the blue is overhead,
   And to good men are good the night and day.

Life's greatest word is but the echo clear
  Of that large heart that knows or loves the most ;
For he that knows is most serene and dear,
  While he that loves may of great knowledge boast.

I know that Death is nothing to the wise
  Who, from the lore collected in his sun
Distils the future with far-seeing eyes,
  And tastes the cup before his day is done.

Descend then, kindly pair, and pluck what flowers
May cheer your path adown the fleeting hours.

A LETTER TO THE CAPE.

DEAR Dick, do leave for once the glare
  Of diamond mines and sandy plains,
The gold, of which you have your share,
  And walk with me in London lanes.

And when we're tired, we'll watch the town,
  Behind a glass of yellow wine,
And lose the patter up and down
  In praise of girls in dresses fine.

Then, as the liquor warms our blood,
  We'll hie us back to boyhood's years
When both our lives were in the bud,
  Bursting with varied hopes and fears.

A parson you were hot to be,
  And now you thrash the nigger's hide ;
Pure science was the aim of me,
  Who on a wayward fancy ride.

But just the same we know the dead—
  My sister, that you loved so well,
Do you remember how she sped
  When she outstripped us down the fell?

And do you mind the water trough
  Where we urged toads in frightened race,

Till she in pity cried *Enough !*
　To us devoid of care and grace?

She's gone : and you and I apart
　Recall the past in fitful word :
The pen but poorly shows the heart ;
　The voice alone can love record.

Come, then, my Dick, and don't be long ;
　I want to hear a private tone.
Each day I see a happy throng,
　But then each day I'm all alone.

POPPIES.

WE saw the farmer's bier
　Borne o'er the golden field ;
The wheat too knew its time was near
　And bent beneath its yield.

We marked the earthy grave
   Whereon, as we came back
To-day, we saw the poppies wave,
   The poppies that he'd hack

And heap upon a pyre,
   Limp, faded green and red,
And blast them utterly with fire.
   Do these now mount the dead?

O gorgers on the past,
   Flap not your bloody wings
Above one foe that's down at last :
   A stronger burns and sings.

AUTUMN.

NOW herbage weary of its crowded fight
   Sinks where the worm awaits a flaccid prey ;
The glories of the expiring reign of light
   Glare a last triumph in the sunflower's ray.

Down creeps the sated snake : silent with dread
    The huddled birds expect the mortal cold,
Save where the robin, careless of his red,
    Pipes in lone melody a tale that's told.

The chill mist deadens sound ; man bears within
    His home, now lighted by the sun's pale ghost,
Memorial thought of what the sun has been
    Through the long summer now for ever lost.

Yet for the herb kind earth protects the seed,
As a loved past the hope of next year's deed.

A GOLDFINCH.

BORN JUNE 1877: DIED 10 SEPTR. 1891.

ON the shaw's tallest tree
    Cradled you were,
Though you ne'er lived to be
    Spurner of air.

Half-fledged and grey you came
   Into our hand
For a life, long and tame,
   In a caged land.

Mays blessed your window-sill,
   Showing heaven's gate :
Mays made your blemished bill
   Immaculate ;

Mays brought a gentle wife
   Bright as your wing,
Warmed you to pride of life
   And carolling.

Daughters and sons you got
   In a long line ;
Envious with them you fought.
   As they grew fine.

Gascon ! did you defy
   Him that fed you,

E

A GOLDFINCH.

While he laughed merrily
  At your brave hue.

You saw our father die
  Loving us well :
Alone flashed your fierce eye
  On him as he fell.

You sang a tiny song
  On the dull morn
That, shrouding the good and strong,
  Left us forlorn.

Yet now your unpaled red,
  And gold of your wing,
We lay with the loved dead,
  Remembering.

MIDDLE AGE.

STEEP years wear fancy out ; at length we stand
   Serene upon the lofty plain to view
   The burial of the brightest face we knew,
And smile maybe : for middle age is bland.

LOVE AND POETRY.

LOVE, the little wingèd lad,
   Came with laughing face to me,
Bound me as I kissed him glad,
Flew away and left me sad,
   Pining for my liberty,
   Naughty, naughty Love to me :

Slowly to my aching side
  Toddled then a baby Muse ;
Lispéd out with tiny pride
" See, the world is very wide ;
  Won't you let me set you loose ? "
How could I the babe refuse.

" Sing a little song to me."
  So I sang a little song,
Pleased with her and glad to see
End to my captivity :
  Love's a short and bitter wrong ;
  Art's a sweet that liveth long.
    Love, Love, away
    For ever and a day !
     Fly, Love !
     Die Love !
    Just as you may,
For you're full of base deceit in all you do and say.

    Muse, live with me ;
    Never care to flee.

> *Prance, sweet,*
> *Dance, sweet,*
> *Ever joyously.*
> *Mine you are, a kinder Love, that made me gay and free.*

MOTHER'S WELL AGAIN.

PROPITIOUS be the fire that bakes
This the last and best of cakes !
Happy we that now have seen it,
For the rarest things are in it—
Thoughts of that long, cakeless time,
When the house without its prime,
Bright controller, chilled and sad,
Threw a gloom o'er lass and lad ;
Thankful glances fell in then
From the mother well again ;
Spice and currant too we see,
Flour and such-like trumpery.
Look ! the mass begins to rise
'Neath the joyful children's eyes,

Surest sign it shall be light
As our hearts are at the sight
Of our queen restored to might.
Soon we'll eat to live and move
Freely in her careful love.

THE CLERKS' FAREWELL

TO THEIR SUPERANNUATED BROTHER,

30, DEC. 1891.

OLD friend, to-night we feel the smart
That burns whenever old friends part.

Maybe that far-off time you mind
When Cornish land you left behind :
Was it not hard to say good-bye
To all the things that pleased your eye—
To white-tails skipping in the furze,
To hedge and ditch, to thorns and burs,
To lilies in the orchard grass,
To cornfield, fellow lad and lass,

To plover flapping o'er the marish,
To partridge crouching in the arrish?
Yet memory of these things was sweet
To you in duty's daily seat,
And tales of happy times by-gone
Helped you to jog with pleasure on
The path of work you've done so well.

And though we heard with pain the knell
That called you from our company,
And often wish that you might be
Still longer with us, yet we know
That kindly speech of you will go
From one to th' other ; what you thought
And did and spoke shall soon be taught
To younger men : and we shall think
Of you, as you of Tamar's brink,
And wish you with your well loved wife
A happy, long and prosperous life.

TO R. K.

THE blackbirds that you sent me
  Were very fine and fit,
But melody of years and miles
  Went fizzle on the spit.

I love a bird's song dearly,
  So next time send me crakes
That night and day o'er woodland tune
  Delight to drag their rakes.

TO MY DOG AND BITCH.

YOU horizontal paupers, late pointing to the pole
Of bread and meat and various mess that makes your daily
     dole,
What mean you now by fixing me with sentimental eye,
As if you had within your ken the matter for a sigh?
You're like the well-fed married dean who wrote a tract to
     show
That old Montaigne though wise enough was lamentably
     low.

TO THIS THIRD BOOK OF MINE.

Number Three,
Go and see
How the world progresses.
Maybe passion
's Out of fashion
And you'll get caresses.

Poets solemn,
On the column
That the mob has raised them
May be sneered at,
Even jeered at
By the crowd that praised them ;

And your prattle,
Silly tattle,

Now may turn some faces
From the preacher
And the teacher
To your tiny graces.

www.ingramcontent.com/pod-product-compliance
Lightning Source LLC
Chambersburg PA
CBHW022206020726
47496CB00008B/2908